Before readir

Look at the book
Ask, "What do you

Level 12 provides   ced
in this series. This   ıding
skills and gives them the confidence to read independently.

During reading

Offer plenty of support and praise as the child reads the story. Listen carefully and respond to events in the text.

All the **Key Words** used in Level 12 have been introduced in earlier stories and will be familiar. If the child hesitates over a word, practise reading it together. If the word is phonically decodable, you can sound out the letters and blend the sounds to read the word ("d-o-g, dog"). Praise the child for their effort, then return to the story.

Pause every few pages and ask questions to check the child's understanding of what they have read. If they begin to lose concentration, stop reading and save the page for later.

Celebrate the child's achievement and come back to the story the next day.

After reading

After reading this book, ask, "Did you enjoy the story? What did you like about it?" Encourage the child to share their opinions.

Use the comprehension questions on page 54 to check the child's understanding and recall of the text.

Ladybird

Series Consultant: Professor David Waugh
With thanks to Kulwinder Maude

LADYBIRD BOOKS

UK | USA | Canada | Ireland | Australia
India | New Zealand | South Africa

Ladybird Books is part of the Penguin Random House group of companies
whose addresses can be found at global.penguinrandomhouse.com.
www.penguin.co.uk   www.puffin.co.uk   www.ladybird.co.uk

 Penguin
Random House
UK

Original edition of Key Words with Peter and Jane first published by Ladybird Books Ltd 1964
Series updated 2023
This book first published 2023
001

Text copyright © Ladybird Books Ltd, 1964, 2023
Illustrations by Pablo Gallego with colour work by Valeria Abatzoglu
Based on characters and design by Gustavo Mazali
Illustrations copyright © Ladybird Books Ltd, 2023

With thanks to Farima Perry for her contributions to the story and illustrations
With thanks to Liz Pemberton for her contributions in advising on the illustrations
With thanks to Inclusive Minds for connecting us with their Inclusion Ambassador network,
and in particular thanks to Guntaas Kaur Chugh for her input on the illustrations

Printed in China

The authorized representative in the EEA is Penguin Random House Ireland,
Morrison Chambers, 32 Nassau Street, Dublin D02 YH68

A CIP catalogue record for this book is available from the British Library

ISBN: 978-0-241-51107-7

All correspondence to:
Ladybird Books
Penguin Random House Children's
One Embassy Gardens, 8 Viaduct Gardens, London SW11 7BW

Key Words

with Peter and Jane

12b

The big wedding

Based on the original
Key Words with Peter and Jane
reading scheme and research by William Murray

Original edition written by William Murray
This edition written by Swapna Haddow
Illustrated by Pablo Gallego with colour work by Valeria Abatzoglu
Based on characters and design by Gustavo Mazali

Peter and Jane were getting ready for Ayan Shah's wedding. Peter, Jane, Mum and Dad were all going, and so was everyone in the street!

Peter and Jane went into Mum and Dad's bedroom to see Ayan's house. There were people putting strings of lights and flowers all over the house. It was fun to see people getting the house ready for the party.

"It looks so pretty," Jane said.

Peter started to count the people at the Shahs' house. For the last three days, many people had come to the house, and the music had been very loud. There had been lots of parties leading up to the big day. It sounded like a lot of fun.

"There must be twenty cars there today!" Peter cried.

Jane didn't think there were that many cars, but she was just as happy as Peter so she didn't say anything. Mum and Dad had asked them to be very good on the day of Ayan's wedding, and Jane wanted to make them proud.

"Come on, Peter and Jane," Mum called up to them. "We're going to be late."

Peter and Jane ran down the stairs, where they were met by Mum. She looked them over, smiling as she brushed them down and checked their clothes. Everyone was in their best clothes, because Mrs Shah had told Mum that this would be a very grand wedding.

Peter's clothes were a bit tight. Mum twisted his tie into place and smoothed his shirt.

"Please don't make a mess of your clothes at the wedding," Mum said to the children. "This is a very big day for Ayan."

Mum used to be Ayan's teacher at school, and Dad now worked with Ayan at the dentist's, so the family knew him well. Jane and Peter sometimes played with Ayan's sister, Sana.

Peter fussed with his hair, while Mum checked Jane's dress.

"Why do we have to put on these clothes?" Peter asked, wishing he could've worn his new robot jumper. "It's just a party."

"It's a wedding!" Jane said. "It's not like a birthday party, you know."

Jane had been to a wedding before, so she had some idea of what Ayan's wedding would be like. Peter didn't remember the other wedding because he was just a baby back then.

"I still think Ayan would like to see my robot jumper," Peter said.

15

When Dad came down the stairs, he had on an outfit that looked just like Peter's! Mum wanted to take some pictures.
She thought Jane looked lovely in her dress, and it was very funny to see Peter and Dad dressed alike.

After they had taken lots of pictures, the family headed over the street to the Shahs' house, which was now covered in lights and flowers.

"This is so fantastic," Jane said, as they joined a stream of people in bright outfits heading into the house.

Tim and Cass Grant were already at the Shahs' with Amber, Will and Maya.

"Hi, Peter!" Amber called. "You look smart."

The door was open, and Peter and Jane could see the house was packed full with the Shahs' friends and family.

"Hello!" Mrs Shah cried, spotting them in the doorway. "Come in, come in!"

Mrs Shah had on a bright blue-and-pink sari. It was covered with pretty gold patterns.

"Seema!" Mum said. "We are so happy for Ayan and your family."

"Thank you so much for having us here today, Seema," Dad said. "We can't wait for the wedding!"

Peter thought that Mrs Shah didn't seem as grumpy as normal. Maybe today was a good day to ask if he could play on the big tree in the Shahs' back garden. "I will ask her later," he thought.

"You look lovely, Seema," Mum said.

"Thank you," Mrs Shah said. "My sister got my sari for me. Come inside and meet her!"

Mum, Dad, Tim and Cass all followed Mrs Shah into the crowd.

"Why don't you all go into the garden?" Mum called to the children.

Peter grinned. Maybe he *would* get to play on the Shahs' big tree today!

Will, Jane, Peter, Amber and Maya headed to the back door. On the way, they saw Ayan laughing and chatting with his friends and family. He looked very smart.

"Where is Sana?" Amber asked.

Ayan spotted the children and waved. "Sana is out in the garden," he told them.

"Isn't it fantastic that we're all part of Ayan's wedding party?" Jane said to the others as they went outside. "It will be great to walk with him to the wedding and to meet the bride's wedding party."

"So these are only *some* of the people going to the wedding?" Peter said. He was very surprised.

"Look! There's Sana," Will said.

Sana was sitting by a big tree. "Grab some juice, and come and sit with me," she called.

Jane and Will poured drinks for everyone, while Peter and Amber ran across the garden to the big tree. Peter had wanted to play on the Shahs' tree for a very long time, but Mrs Shah always said no. She said that she didn't want him to fall.

"Don't, Peter," Jane said. "You know what Mum said about making a mess of your clothes."

Peter grabbed the lowest branch of the tree and pulled himself up. He could see now that the other branches were higher than he'd first thought. The branches also weren't as strong as they looked. "Maybe Mrs Shah was right," he thought.

"Do you need a hand?" Sana asked.

"Yes, please," Peter said.

Sana grabbed Peter's foot to help him. But, as Peter went to swing his leg over the branch, he bumped Will's arm with his foot, and Will fell into Jane.

"My dress!" Jane cried, as her drink splashed all over it.

"Oh no! Sorry, Will!" Peter said. "I'm really sorry, Jane." Amber ran to the table to get some napkins.

33

"Mum is going to be so upset!" Jane cried, dabbing a napkin on the stain on her dress.

"Quick, let's go back to our house so you can put on a new dress," Peter said, getting down from the tree. "I don't want to upset Mum."

But it was too late. Mum had seen Amber run to the table for napkins. She'd asked Amber what had happened, and she had seen what was going on by the big tree.

"Oh, Jane," Mum said, rushing over. "You'll have to get some clean clothes. You can't stay in a stained dress all day."

Mrs Shah came outside to see what all the fuss was about. When Mum told her, she gave Peter a stern look.

"I'll have to take Jane home to get her some clean clothes," Mum said. "I'm sorry about this, Seema."

"Sana has lots of lovely clothes that are too small for her now," said Mrs Shah. "I bet we can find a dress for Jane."

"But you have so much to do today!" said Mum.

"Come with me quickly, Jane, and we'll find something," Mrs Shah said.

Mrs Shah took Jane's hand and led her into the house to find her some clean clothes. "Sana, you can help too," she said.

Jane, Sana and Mrs Shah went into Sana's bedroom. Mrs Shah looked through Sana's clothes, and laid outfits on the bed for Jane. The clothes were all very colourful, with shimmering beads and patterns.

"What do you think of this one, Jane?" Sana asked.

She pointed to a long yellow skirt with gold patterns and beads. Next to it was a gold top and a shawl.

"I got this outfit for another family wedding," Sana said to Jane.

"I really like it," Jane said. "Can I try it on, please?"

Sana nodded. "I'll help you," she said.

Jane had fun trying on lots of Sana's old clothes, but Mrs Shah was still looking through them.

"I found it!" Mrs Shah cried suddenly, reaching up to a high shelf. She pulled down a bright pink box.

Jane opened the box. Inside, there was a blue-and-silver outfit. "I love it!" she said, grinning at Mrs Shah.

"You can put on this necklace with it," Sana said.

Jane showed everyone her new wedding clothes.

"You look great!" said Peter.

Two of Sana's family friends came over to see Jane's outfit. They had flower patterns on their hands and arms.

"Do you like our henna tattoos?" they asked.

"Yes, I do," said Jane.

"Someone drew the patterns on their skin with henna paste," Sana told Jane. "Mira, the bride, will have henna tattoos too."

"They are lovely," Jane said.

Will and Peter spotted a table covered with bright boxes.

"Wow!" said Will. "That is a lot of presents."

Mr Shah joined them. "I see you've found the gifts!" he said to the boys.

"Are they all for Ayan and Mira?" asked Peter.

"No, they are for Mira's family. The groom's family take gifts for the bride's family to the wedding," Mr Shah told them.

Suddenly, there was loud music outside.

"I can hear drumming!" said Will.

Mr Shah clapped his hands. "It's time!"

"The drummers are here to walk with Ayan and his family to the wedding," Dad said to Will and Peter. "And we get to walk with them too."

Everyone walked as a group from the Shahs' house. The drummers drummed and everyone sang!

Peter and Jane walked with Amber and Will, and they all laughed and sang along.

The wedding room was lit up with lots of lights and covered with flowers. Ayan sat down, and soon the bride, Mira, and her family and friends arrived.

Jane liked it when Ayan and Mira gave each other flower garlands.

Peter could smell all the fantastic food that was cooking in the kitchen down the hall. He suddenly felt very hungry.

After the wedding, everyone sat down to eat dinner.

The children had lots of fun trying out different dishes. Some people handed out sweets at the children's table.

"Would you like something to drink, Jane?" Peter asked, holding up a jug.

"No, thanks," Jane said, laughing. "Keep that juice away from me!"

The party went on all through the night, and Peter and Jane agreed it was the best wedding ever!

Questions

Answer these questions about the story.

1 Who is getting married in this story?

2 What does Peter wish he could wear to the wedding?

3 What is Mrs Shah wearing at the wedding? Who got it for her?

4 How do you think Peter feels when Jane's drink splashes on her dress?

5 Where does Jane get clean wedding clothes from?

6 How do Jane and Peter get to the wedding? What do they do along the way?